The Pirate TREASURE

BY MICHÈLE DUFRESNE

CONTENTS

Pioneer Valley Educational Press, Inc.

chapter one

THE TREASURE MAP

Jack and Daisy were playing with a ball.

"Fetch it, Jack!" said Daisy. She pushed the ball, and the ball rolled under a bush.

Jack ran to get the ball. "Look, Daisy. There's something under this bush! What is it?"

Daisy ran over and looked under the bush.
"It's a map!" said Daisy.

"What's a map?" asked Jack.
"Can I eat it?"

"No!" said Daisy.
"You can't eat a map.
A map can show you how to find places."

Daisy looked at the map.
"I think this map is a treasure map," she told Jack.

"A treasure map?
What's a treasure map?"
asked Jack.

"It's a map that shows you
where to find buried treasure,"
said Daisy.

"Oh!" said Jack. "This is exciting!
Buried treasure! Like from a pirate?
Can the map help us
find the buried treasure?"

"I think so," said Daisy.

"See the **X** on the map?

I think that's where the treasure

is buried."

"I can't wait to see the treasure.
I wonder what the pirates buried!"
said Jack.

"OK," said Daisy. "We just need
to follow the map! Let's go!"

"First, I need my pirate hat,"
said Jack. "I will wear my pirate hat
so the pirates know
I am a pirate, too!"

"Can I wear your Super Dog cape?"
asked Daisy. "It might help me
find the treasure."

"No!" said Jack. "Today, we will be pirates. Do you have a pirate hat?"

"No," said Daisy sadly. "I just have dresses."

"I think some pirates wear dresses," said Jack.

"They do?" said Daisy. "OK, I will wear a dress then."

chapter two
LOOKING FOR TREASURE

Jack put on his pirate hat.
Daisy put on a dress.

"Come on. The map tells us
to go up the driveway
and into the woods," said Daisy.

"Oh, dear," said Jack.
"What if there are foxes or bears?
Maybe we should get Bella
and Rosie to come with us."

"No!" said Daisy. "They think we are too little to do big things. We found the map. We can find the treasure by ourselves!"

"We can?" asked Jack.

"Yes! Let's go!" said Daisy.

Daisy and Jack walked all the way up the driveway until they came to a road. Just then, Bella ran out from the woods.

"Where are you going?" asked Bella.

"Oh . . . we are just going for a walk," said Daisy.

"Well, what's that?" asked Bella. "Is that a treasure map? Are you looking for buried treasure?"

"It's OUR map," said Daisy.
"And you can't come."

"OK, but you are going the wrong way," said Bella.

"We are going the wrong way?" said Jack. "Oh, dear."

"If you let me share the treasure,
I'll help you find it," said Bella.

"OK," said Daisy.

"Follow me," said Bella.
Bella, Daisy, and Jack
walked back down the driveway
and into the woods.

"Come on, follow me," said Bella.
"The buried treasure is this way."

"I think the treasure
is buried here," said Bella.
"Let's dig it up!"

Daisy and Bella began to dig.

Jack looked around.
"I hear something," he said.

"I don't hear anything," said Daisy.
"Help us dig up the treasure!"

"Listen!" said Jack. "What's that?
Is that a fox or a bear? Oh, no!
Maybe it's a pirate!"

Just then Rosie ran up.
"What are you doing?" she asked.

"Just digging," said Daisy.

"Hey!" said Rosie.
"You have my map!"

"Your map?" said Bella.

"It's a treasure map," said Jack.
"A pirate made it. We are looking for buried treasure."

"There's no pirate treasure," said Rosie.

"There isn't pirate treasure here?" asked Jack.

"No pirate treasure," said Rosie.
"But look, there are four bones,
one for each of us."

"Hooray! Bones!" said Jack and Daisy.

"Thank you for finding my map,"
said Rosie. "I lost it, and then
I couldn't find my bones!"